LAFF-O-TRONIC

PRESENTS

A SUPER-TERRIFIC COLLECTION OF **JOKES, COMICS, GAGS,** AND BASICALLY EVERYTHING CRAZY AND STRANGE AND COOL ABOUT...

SCHOOL!

BORING STUFF...

LAFF-O-TRONIC JOKE BOOKS! IS PUBLISHED
BY STONE ARCH BOOKS, A CAPSTONE IMPRINT
1710 ROE CREST DRIVE
NORTH MANKATO, MN 56003
WWW.CAPSTONEYOUNGREADERS.COM

CATALOGING-IN-PUBLICATION DATA IS AVAILABLE
ON THE LIBRARY OF CONGRESS WEBSITE.
ISBN: 978-1-4342-6022-2 (LIBRARY HARDCOVER)
ISBN: 978-1-4342-6192-2 (PAPERBACK)

DESIGNER: RUSSELL GRIESMER
EDITOR: DONALD LEMKE

PRINTED IN THE UNITED STATES OF AMERICA
IN STEVENS POINT, WISCONSIN.
082013   007679R

LAFF-O-TRONIC

SCHOOL JOKES!

BY
"ASSISTANT PRINCIPAL OF CLASS CLOWNING"
MICHAEL DAHL!!

ILLUSTRATED BY

**DARYLL COLLINS
AND DOUG HOLGATE**

STONE ARCH BOOKS™
a capstone imprint

PRESS TO START!

FYI: THIS IS A BOOK. BUTTONS DON'T WORK IN BOOKS. YOU WILL PROBABLY HAVE TO TURN THE PAGE.

When is a school bus not a school bus?
When it turns into a parking lot!

What school contest did the skunk win?
The smelling bee.

Why did the computer teacher keep a spider in her classroom?
Because it was so good at making websites.

How did the music teacher fix the broken tuba?

With a tuba glue.

Why was Cinderella thrown off the soccer team?

Because she ran away from the ball.

Why was Cinderella so bad at gymnastics?
Because she had a pumpkin for a coach.

**Why did the teacher
wear sunglasses?**

His class was so bright.

Why are fish so smart?
Because they live in schools.

**Why did the girl put on lipstick
during the test?**

The teacher was giving a make-up exam.

Why isn't there a clock in the school library?

It tocks too much.

What's brown, goes to school, and lives in a bell tower?

The Lunch Bag of Notre Dame.

Did you hear about the cross-eyed teacher?

He couldn't control his pupils!

Why did the science teacher put a knocker on the classroom door?

She wanted to win the no-bell prize.

What's the geometry teacher's favorite dessert?

Pi.

In what school do you have to drop out to graduate?

Sky-diving.

Why did the teacher raise all the chairs in his classroom?

He wanted to keep his students on their toes.

What did the mother buffalo say when her boy went off to school?

"Bison."

Why did the girl eat her history test?

The teacher said it was a piece of cake.

What kind of food do math teachers eat?

Square meals.

How did the little squid get to school?

He took the octobus!

Why did the clock in the cafeteria run slow?
Because every lunch it went back four seconds.

**What does an elf work on when
he gets home from school?**
His gnomework.

What has sixty feet and sings?
The school choir.

Why did the porcupine join the debate team?
He was always good at making a poinl.

Why did the student have a flashlight in his lunch box?
He wanted a light snack.

Why did the music teacher send the girl to the principal's office?
She was a treblemaker.

**What did the paper clip
say to the magnet?**

**What did the sheet of paper say
to the noisy scissors?**

What did the calculator say to the student?

What did the eraser say to the talkative thumb tack?

What did the glue say to the glitter?

What did the lunch bag say to the banana?

What did the eraser say to the near-sighted student?

What did the pencil say to the piece of paper?

What did the math book say to the science book?

What did the pen say to the measuring stick?

MORE JOKES!

Did you hear about the strawberries that started a school band?

They just got together and jammed!

Where does the third grade come AFTER the fourth grade?

In the dictionary.

What animals are the best teachers?
Skunks. They make the most scents.

What do you call a student with a dictionary in his pocket?
A smarty pants.

What did the ghost teacher say to her class?
"Look at the board, and I'll go through it again."

Why did the nurse fail at art class?
She could only draw blood.

What did the little turtles say to their teacher?

"You tortoise everything we know."

What's a snake's favorite class?

Hisssssssstory!

Did you hear the balloon got the best grade on the test?

Yeah, it rose to the top of the class!

Why was the cheese afraid of going to school?

It didn't want to be grated!

Why did the thermometer go to school?
It wanted to gain a degree.

What do you call a duck who always gets good grades?
A wise quacker.

What's a soda pop's favorite class?
Fizz Ed.

Why did the spoon have to stay after school?
He was always stirring up trouble.

Why was the little kid late for school?

Because there's eight in his family, but the alarm clock was only set for seven.

Why did the Cyclops stop teaching?

He only had one pupil!

What vegetable do librarians like?
Quiet peas!

What is a pirate's favorite school subject?
Arrrrrrrt!

Why did the music teacher get locked out of the classroom?

Because his keys were on the piano.

Why didn't the sun go to school?

It already had a million degrees!

What do you call a pirate who skips school?

Captain Hooky.

Why are kindergarten teachers always so optimistic?

Because every day they make little things count.

**Who keeps track of all the meals
in the school cafeteria?**

The lunch counter.

**Why did the math teacher put
a ruler in her bed?**

She wanted to see how long she slept!

**Did you know that all the books in the
library are the same color?**

Really?

Yeah, they're all red.

**What did the computer
do at lunchtime?**

It had a byte.

Why was the kid's report card all wet?
It was below C level!

What student likes lying in front of the school door?

MAT

What student likes to hang on the wall?

ART

What student loves to eat hamburgers?

PATTY

What student likes to go rock climbing?

CLIFF

What student is good at playing tennis?

ANNETTE

What student is good at floating in the swimming pool?

BOB

What student is good to have around auto repair class?

JACK

What student can you find in the lunchroom?

STU

What student used to like art class?

DREW

What student is always hanging around the principal?

TY

Who invented King Arthur's famous round table?

Sir Cumference.

Where did Sir Lancelot learn to kill dragons?

At knight school.

Who invented fractions?

Henry the 1/8.

Did Native Americans ever hunt bear?

Not in the winter, they didn't!

**How did Columbus's men
sleep on their ships?**

With their eyes shut.

**Where did the Pilgrims land
when they first arrived in
the New World?**

On their feet.

**Where was the Declaration
of Independence signed?**

At the bottom!

**Why was George Washington
buried at Mount Vernon?**

Because he was dead.

What did George Washington say after he chopped down the cherry tree?

I'm stumped.

Where can you find the Great Plains?

In a great airport.

Why does the Statue of Liberty stand in New York Harbor?

Because it can't sit down?

Do you know the 20th president of the United States?

No, we were never introduced.

Teacher: Who was Joan of Arc?
Student: Noah's wife?

Teacher: How did the Vikings send messages to one another?

Student: They used Norse code.

What did they wear at the Boston Tea Party?

Tea shirts.

ARITHMETIC TEACHER

ADAM UPP

SCIENCE TEACHER

TESS TOOB

ART TEACHER

DREW LOTTS

GYM TEACHER

FLETCHER BYSEPPS

BIOLOGY TEACHER

ANN ADDA MEE

CHOIR TEACHER

LOWDEN KLEER

CHEMISTRY TEACHER

MACON STOFF

MUSIC TEACHER

TRISTAN SHOWT

DANCE TEACHER

COREY O'GRAFF

LANGUAGE ARTS TEACHER

REED ENRIGHT

GEOMETRY TEACHER

POLLY GONE

ASTRONOMY TEACHERS

LUKE N. DESKYE & SEYMOUR STARRS

GERMAN TEACHER

ALFIE DURR ZAYNE

COOKING CLASS TEACHER

X. BENEDICT

This MUST be some kind of joke!

MORE JOKES?!

What happened when the teacher tied the students' shoelaces together?

They all took a class trip!

Principal: I've had to punish you every day this week, Robert. What do you have to say for yourself?

Robert: I'm glad it's Friday!

KID #1: "Did you read that book about Henry Ford?"

KID #2: "Yeah, it was an auto-biography."

Teacher: "Amy, what's a metaphor?"

Amy: "It's for cows to stand around in."

Teacher: "What do they raise during the rainy season in Peru?"

Student: "Umbrellas!"

Teacher: "Where can you find the Red Sea?"

Donnie: "Usually on my report card!"

Why did the nose not want to go to school?

It was tired of getting picked on!

What's the worst thing about the school cafeteria?

The food!

How do you get straight A's?
By using a ruler!

What did you learn at school today?
Not enough, I have to go back tomorrow!

Mother: "I don't think my child deserves a zero on this test."
Teacher: "Neither do I, but it's the lowest score I can give!"

Teacher: "Why is the Mississippi River so famous?"

Student: "Because it has four eyes and still can't see?"

Teacher: "Can you use the word 'fascinate' in a sentence?"

Beth: "Yes, my jacket has eight buttons but I can only fasten eight."

Teacher: "Do you know the capital of Alaska?"

Student: "Juneau."

Teacher: "Well, of course I know, young man, but I'm asking you!"

What do librarians take with them when they go fishing?

Bookworms!

Kid #1: "Why are you crying?"

Kid #2: "The teacher told me to go straight home after school."

Kid #1: "So?"

Kid #2: "I can't. I live around the corner!"

Teacher: "What is the subordinate claus?"

Kid: "One of Santa's elves?"

Kid #1: "Are you any good at math?"

Kid #2: "Yes and no."

Kid #1: "What do you mean?"

Kid #2: "I mean yes. I'm no good at math."

Teacher: "I see you missed school yesterday."
Student: "No, not really."

Teacher: "I hope I didn't see you copying your neighbor's test."
Student: "I hope you didn't either!"

Astronomy teacher: "Is it ever possible for us to see new stars?"
Kid: "Sure! Go to Hollywood."

Teacher: "Did your parents help you with this homework?"

Student: "No. I got it all wrong by myself."

Knock, knock.

Who's there?

Me.

Me who?

No, seriously, it's just me. I am telling a knock-knock joke.

Knock, knock.

Who's there?

Police.

Police who?

Police stop telling these terrible jokes!

Knock, knock.

Who's there?

General Lee.

General Lee who?

General Lee I don't tell stupid knock-knock jokes!

Knock, knock.

Who's there?

Shirley.

Shirley who?

Shirley you know better jokes than these!

Knock, knock.

Who's there?

Claire.

Claire who?

Claire the way, I'm coming through!

BOY: "I guess this is what Coach means by being motivated."

TEACHER: "The first step in the procedure, class, is to remove your specimen from the jar."

A Visit to the Museum

This, class, is a man-eating Tiger!

Ooohh! Aaah!

Knock, knock.
Who's there?
Ben.
Ben who?
Ben looking all over for you!

Knock, knock.
Who's there?
Sherwood.
Sherwood who?
Sherwood be nice to come inside!

Knock, knock.
Who's there?
Boo.
Boo who?
Well you don't have to cry about it!

Knock, knock.
Who's there?
Watson.
Watson who?
Watson TV tonight?

Knock, knock.
Who's there?
Anita.
Anita who?
Anita come in - it's raining!

Knock, knock.
Who's there?
Justin.
Justin who?
Justin time for dinner.

Knock, knock.
Who's there?
Hatch.
Hatch who?
Will ya please cover up when you sneeze?!

Knock, knock.
Who's there?
Cash.
Cash who?
No thanks, but I'd love a peanut!

Knock Knock.
Who's there?
Avenue.
Avenue who?
Avenue heard this joke before.

Knock, knock.
Who's there?
Cows go.
Cows go who?
No, cows go moo.

Knock, knock.
Who's there?
Lettuce.
Lettuce who?
Lettuce in! It's cold out here!

Knock, knock.
Who's there?
Radio.
Radio who?
Radio or not, here I come!

Knock, knock.

Who's there?

Zombies.

Zombies who?

Zombies make honey, and zombies don't.

Knock, knock.

Who's there?

Thermos.

Thermos who?

Thermos be a better knock-knock joke than that last one!

Knock, knock.

Who's there?

Tank.

Tank who?

You're welcome!

Knock, knock.
Who's there?
Annie.
Annie who?
Annie body home?

Knock, knock.
Who's there?
Alex.
Alex who?
Alex plain later.

Knock, knock.
Who's there?
Doris.
Doris who?
**Doris locked, that's
why I'm knocking.**

Knock, knock.
Who's there?
Butter.
Butter who?
**Butter open the door quick,
I need to use the bathroom!**

Knock, knock.
Who's there?
Wanda.
Wanda who?
**Wanda door opens I'll
stop da knocking.**

Knock, knock.
Who's there?
Abby.
Abby who?
Abby Birthday to you!

It Screams At Midnight, by Waylon Moan

I Was A Teenage Werewolf, by Anita Shave

Attack of the Zombies, by Doug Moregraves

The Phantom Strangler, by Hans Archer Throte

Don't Go Out At Night! by Freyda Thudark

The Fortune Teller, by Horace Cope

Chased by the Wolfman, by Claude S. Armoff

Invisible Ink, by M. T. Pages

The Hunchback of Notre Dame, by Isabelle Ringing

The Eyes of Medusa, by May Dove Stone

Aliens Have Landed! by Ross Well

A Zombie's Life, by Myra Maines

Making New Things, by N. Ventor

In the Laboratory, by Tess Tube

The World of the Unknown, by Misty Rees

Beware the Bride of Frankenstein, by Sheila Tack

Easy Recipes for the Busy Zombie, by Hugh Mann Bings

Into the Haunted House, by Hugo First

FLIPPIN' OUT!

Marching Brat

1. Grab the bottom-right corner of page 79.

2. Flip page 79 back and forth without letting go.

3. Keep an eye on page 81.

4. If you flip fast enough, pages 79 and 81 will look like one, animated picture!

FLippin' OUT!

Apple of Her AYEEE!

1. Grab the bottom-right corner of page 83.

2. Flip page 83 back and forth without letting go.

3. Keep an eye on page 85.

4. If you flip fast enough, pages 83 and 85 will look like one, animated picture!

FLippin' OUT!

Dodge This!

1. Grab the bottom-right corner of page 87.

2. Flip page 87 back and forth without letting go.

3. Keep an eye on page 89.

4. If you flip fast enough, pages 87 and 89 will look like one, animated picture!

How to Draw
A Wacky Pencil!

(YOU'LL NEED A PENCIL, A PIECE OF PAPER, AND AN ERASER.)

1. USING YOUR PENCIL, DRAW THE SIDES OF YOUR WACKY PENCIL, AS SHOWN AT RIGHT.

2. THEN ADD THE PENCIL'S POINTED TIP AND ERASER.

3. NEXT, GIVE YOUR WACKY PENCIL AN EXTRA LOOOOONG NOSE!

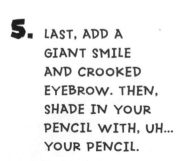

4. THEN DRAW TWO SMALL CIRCLES FOR EYEBALLS. MAKE SURE THE EYES LINE UP ON THE ERASER LINE. DON'T FORGET THE PUPILS!

5. LAST, ADD A GIANT SMILE AND CROOKED EYEBROW. THEN, SHADE IN YOUR PENCIL WITH, UH... YOUR PENCIL.

AUTHOR

MICHAEL DAHL

HAS WRITTEN MORE THAN 200 BOOKS FOR YOUNG READERS. HE IS THE AUTHOR OF THE SUPER-FUNNY JOKE BOOKS SERIES, *THE EVERYTHING KIDS' JOKE BOOKS,* THE SCINTILLATING *DUCK GOES POTTY,* AND TWO HUMOROUS MYSTERY SERIES: FINNEGAN ZWAKE (A "WISECRACKING RIOT" ACCORDING TO THE *CHICAGO TRIBUNE*) AND HOCUS POCUS HOTEL. HE TOURED THE COUNTRY WITH AN IMPROV TROUPE, AND BEGAN HIS AUSPICIOUS COMIC CAREER IN 5TH GRADE WHEN HIS STAND-UP ROUTINE MADE HIS MUSIC TEACHER LAUGH SO HARD SHE FELL OFF HER CHAIR. SHE IS NOT AVAILABLE FOR COMMENT.

ILLUSTRATORS

DOUGLAS HOLGATE

IS A FREELANCE ILLUSTRATOR, COMIC BOOK ARTIST, AND CARTOONIST BASED IN MELBOURNE, AUSTRALIA. HIS WORK HAS BEEN PUBLISHED ALL AROUND THE WORLD BY RANDOM HOUSE, SIMON AND SCHUSTER, THE NEW YORKER MAGAZINE, MAD MAGAZINE, IMAGE COMICS, AND MANY OTHERS. HIS WORKS FOR CHILDREN INCLUDE THE ZINC ALLOY AND BIKE RIDER SERIES (CAPSTONE), SUPER CHICKEN NUGGET BOY (HYPERION), AND A NEW SERIES OF POPULAR SCIENCE BOOKS BY DR. KARL KRUSZELNICKI (PAN MACMILLAN). DOUGLAS HAS SPORTED A POWERFUL, MANLY BEARD SINCE AGE 12 (PROBABLY NOT TRUE) AND IS ALSO A PRETTY RAD DUDE (PROBABLY TRUE).

DARYLL COLLINS

IS A FREELANCE CARTOONIST WHOSE WORK HAS APPEARED IN BOOKS, MAGAZINES, COMIC STRIPS, ADVERTISING, GREETING CARDS, PRODUCT PACKAGING AND CHARACTER DESIGN. HE ENJOYS MUSIC, MOVIES, BASEBALL, FOOTBALL, COFFEE, PIZZA, PETS, AND OF COURSE... CARTOONS!

THE FUN DOESN'T STOP HERE!
DISCOVER MORE AT...

www.CapstoneKids.com